key to reading™

At Key Porter Kids, we understand how important reading is to a young child's development. That's why we created the Key to Reading program, a structured approach to reading for the beginner. While the books in this series are educational, they are also engaging and fun – key elements in gaining and retaining a child's interest. Plus, with each level in the program designed for different reading abilities, children can advance at their own pace and become successful, confident readers in the process.

Level 1: The Beginner

For children familiar with the alphabet and ready to begin reading.

- Very large type
- Simple words
- Short sentences
- Repetition of key words
- Picture cues
- Colour associations
- Directional reading
- Picture match-up cards

Level 2: The Emerging Reader

For children able to recognize familiar words on sight and sound out new words with help.

- Large type
- Easy words
- Longer sentences
- Repetition of key words and phrases
- Picture cues
- Context cues
- Directional reading
- Picture and word match-up cards

Level 3: The Independent Reader

For increasingly confident readers who can sound out new words on their own.

- Large type
- Expanded vocabulary
- Longer sentences and paragraphs
- Repetition of longer words and phrases
- Picture cues
- Context cues
- More complex storylines
- Flash cards

Ruby wanted to take a family picture.
Max wanted to chase a butterfly.

"You can't chase a butterfly," said Ruby. "I'm going to take a picture for Grandma."

Ruby got the camera ready.
Max sat down by a tree.
He got hungry.

He nibbled on an orange candy.
Suddenly, a butterfly flew by.
"Butterfly," said Max.

"Okay, Max," said Ruby.
"The camera is ready."
But Max was chasing the butterfly!

"Watch your orange candy!" yelled Ruby.
"You'll mess up your blue shirt."
But it was too late.

Orange candy got on Max's clothes.
"Oh, no," said Ruby.
"You can't look like that in the picture."

Max put on a clean blue shirt.
"This looks great," said Ruby.
"I'll get the camera ready."

Suddenly, the butterfly flew by again. "Butterfly," said Max.

Max chased the butterfly toward Ruby.
Ruby pressed the camera button.
"Click" went the camera.

The picture was ruined.
"We've only one shot left," said Ruby.
"We have to get it right this time."

Suddenly, the butterfly flew by again.
"Butterfly," said Max.

Max chased the butterfly.
He ran through a puddle.
Mud splashed on Ruby's dress.

"I can't have a mud stain," said Ruby.
Then she got an idea.
Ruby put flowers over the mud.

"Come on, Max," said Ruby.
"Get ready. Say cheese!"

Just then, the butterfly landed on Ruby.
"Butterfly," said Max.
"Click" went the camera.

Ruby and Max went to Grandma's house.
They gave her the picture.

"What a beautiful picture," said Grandma.
"I really love the..."

"Butterfly," said Max.